BAKUGAN

BATTLE BRAWLERS

A DOUBLE BATTLE

BY TRACEY WEST

SCHOLASTIC INC.

NEW YORK   TORONTO   LONDON   AUCKLAND   SYDNEY
MEXICO CITY   NEW DELHI   HONG KONG   BUENOS AIRES

No part of this publication may be reproduced in whole or in part, or stored in a retrieval system, or transmitted in any form or by any means, electronic, mechanical, photocopying, recording, or otherwise, without written permission of the publisher. For information regarding permission, write to Scholastic Inc., Attention: Permissions Department, 557 Broadway, New York, NY 10012.

ISBN-13: 978-0-545-12100-2
ISBN-10: 0-545-12100-0

© Spin Master Ltd/Sega Toys.

BAKUGAN and BATTLE BRAWLERS, and all related titles, logos, and characters are trademarks of Spin Master Ltd. Nelvana is a trademark of Nelvana Limited. Corus is a trademark of Corus Entertainment Inc. Used under license by Scholastic Inc. All Rights Reserved.

Published by Scholastic Inc. SCHOLASTIC and associated logos are trademarks and/or registered trademarks of Scholastic Inc.

12 11 10 9 8 7 6 5 4 3 2 1   9 10 11 12/0

Cover designed by TK
Interior designed by TK
Printed in the U.S.A.
First printing, January 2009

CHAPTER 1

A BRAWLING BULLY

Dan Kuso leaned back in his chair. His Bakugan Drago was perched on the desk in front of him.

It was Saturday morning, and Dan was busy talking with his Bakugan friends on the Internet. His whole life had changed the day Bakugan cards began to fall from the sky. Dan and his friends invented a game with the cards . . . and then one day, the game had become real.

Bakugan lived in another dimension called Vestroia. Not long ago, the wall between Vestroia and the human world was ripped apart. Now Dan's Dragonoid Bakugan was a real beast named Drago who could talk, think, and act on his own.

"Actually, Dan, I'm surprised Drago sticks with you," his friend Runo said. Her face appeared in a corner of Dan's screen via video cam, while images of Dan's other friends filled the remainder. "I know how you can be sometimes . . ."

Dan was insulted. "Hey! Like you're one to talk, Runo. You don't know how to treat a Bakugan!"

Runo looked at the white and gold Bakugan in her palm. "Oh yeah? We get along just fine, Dan."

"I must admit, she treats me rather well," Tigrerra agreed.

Runo smiled. "Ah, isn't she a little cutie?"

"Sorry to interrupt," piped up Maruchan from the computer screen. The small boy had yellow hair and big eyeglasses. "We need to focus on Masquerade. He threatens all of us with his scheme to steal our Bakugan."

Dan knew Maruchan was right. The mysterious masked brawler called Masquerade was brawling kids everywhere and winning. He even played with a card that sent losing Bakugan into the terrible Doom Dimension! Both Dan and Runo had already faced Masquerade — and lost.

But before he could start strategizing with his friends, he heard his mom's voice outside his door.

"Dan, are you in there?"

Dan didn't reply. She probably had some chores from him to do — and he had Bakugan business to take care of.

His mom burst into the room. "Dan, why didn't you answer me?"

Dan shrugged. "Gee, Mom, I guess I didn't hear you."

"Well, I have a little job for you do to," she said. She held a shopping bag in her hand.

"But I'm busy right now!" Dan protested. "You're killin' my chillin' time."

"I need you to scoot on over to the supermarket," Dan's mom said firmly. "Grocery Town is having a sale on loin tips — your favorite!" She held up a flyer with a picture of chunks of juicy beef.

Dan suddenly changed his mind. "Ahhh, sweet! We haven't had them in months!"

Soon Dan was marching to Grocery Town, singing as he went.

"Loin tips, loin tips, eat them up, yum!"

Inside Dan's pocket, Drago sighed. "I will never understand humans!"

In a nearby park, three boys huddled under a shady tree. One of the boys held a box full of Bakugan. The colorful Bakugan balls rolled around in the box.

"Whoa, cool!" the other two boys said.

"Yeah, I'm pretty proud of them myself," said the boy holding the Bakugan.

Suddenly, a boy came out of nowhere and kicked the Bakugan out of his hand.

"What'd you do that for?" the boy asked.

The bully grinned. He had brown eyes and wavy

purple hair. He wore a sleeveless green vest and yellow pants.

"Maybe 'cause I like it!" the bully replied. "Besides, you're too young to be messin' with Bakugans."

One of the boys made a fist, trying to look tough. "Why don't you beat it?" he said.

"No, you should beat it!" the bully shouted back, lunging at them. The frightened younger boys scattered.

"That's it, run home to mommy!" the bully called after them.

Then he noticed something. A boy sat on a branch in the tree. He wore a blue mask over his eyes and a long, white coat over purple pants.

"What's up with the costume?" the bully asked.

"My name is Masquerade," the stranger calmly replied.

"That's nice. Who cares?" the bully shot back.

Masquerade smiled like a snake ready to swallow a mouse. "It appears you think you're quite the Bakugan Brawler," he said. "So are you willing to test your mettle, Tatsuya?"

"How did you know my name?" Tatsuya asked.

Masquerade just smiled. "Well?" he asked.

Tatsuya grinned. "Bring it!"

Masquerade jumped down from the tree. The two brawlers faced each other. Each one held up a Bakugan card.

"Bakugan Field Open!" they yelled.

CHAPTER 2

CENTIPOID STRIKES

The park melted away around them as Masquerade dropped a strange-looking card. It sank into the field and disappeared in a glow of purple light.

Then each brawler threw down a Gate Card. The facedown cards lined up end to end between the boys.

Tatsuya held up a red and gold Bakugan ball. "Guess it's my turn!" he cried. "Bakugan Brawl!"

He threw out the ball, which rolled onto the Gate Card nearest Masquerade. When the ball stopped rolling, Tatsuya yelled out, "Bakugan Stand!"

The ball transformed into a Bakugan that looked like a large snake — a Serpenoid. The red and gold beast was a Pyrus Bakugan, which gave it fiery energy and strength.

"You don't stand a chance against my Mantris!" Tatsuya bragged.

Masquerade laughed to himself. *Nicely played. His*

Mantris has fire attributes. But he's not nearly strong enough.

"I think it's time to exterminate your Mantris," Masquerade called out. "Bakugan Brawl!"

Masquerade threw out a purple and black Bakugan ball. It landed on the Gate Card in front of Tatsuya, behind Serpenoid.

"Bakugan Stand!" Masquerade cried.

The Bakugan transformed into Fear Ripper, a humanoid creature wearing black and midnight-blue body armor and a black mask that covered his whole face. A purple cape hung down his back, and he held a long-handled weapon with a sharp double blade at the end. Fear Ripper was a Darkus Bakugan, a type known for their destructive power.

"Ooh, I'm so scared," Tatsuya said. "Like your overgrown tin can has a chance! How shall I counter?"

First Tatsuya threw out another Gate Card, which landed next to the card Fear Ripper stood on. Then he tossed out a red and gold Bakugan Ball. "Bakugan Brawl!"

The ball rolled onto the new Gate Card.

"Bakugan Stand!" Tatsuya yelled.

The ball transformed into a Pyrus Stingslash. The red beast looked like a scorpion with huge, orange pincers, stinging orange tail, and a creepy human-like face.

Tatsuya grinned, pleased with his move. *Okay, my Gate Card gives me another 200 Gs, so that brings my Stingslash up to 560 Gs. That should do it.*

"Your move!" he called out.

Masquerade smirked and threw out a Gate Card. "Gate Card Set!" The card lined up end to end with the third card on the field, forming a square of four cards.

Then he tossed another purple and black Bakugan Ball on the field. It landed on the new Gate Card.

"Bakugan Brawl!" he yelled.

The ball transformed into a Darkus Centipoid, a beast with a long black body, lots of wiggling legs, and two fangs coming from its mouth.

"Ha!" Tatsuya laughed. "That's what you call a counter move? You're going down in the first round, creep!"

Masquerade held up another card. "Not after I throw this down. Ability Card Activate!"

He grunted as he hurled the card into the dark sky above the field. It disappeared in a flash of light.

"I'm in trouble," Tatsuya said.

Jagged streaks of purple lightning rained down from the sky.

"You talk big. But can you back it up, punk?" Masquerade asked.

The lightning zapped Centipoid, and the strike seemed to energize the beast. Then the electric waves reached out and grabbed Serpenoid and Stingslash like sizzling fingers. It dragged the two Bakugan onto the card with Centipoid.

Tatsuya wasn't worried. "Ha! My Mantris and Stingslash are gonna eat your Bakugan for breakfast!"

Masquerade shook his head. "You do know who you're dealing with, don't you? Gate Card Open!"

A green and blue light swirled around the Gate Card. Centipoid reared up, charged with extra G power.

It attacked Mantris first, lunging forward and grasping the beast's neck between its fangs. Then it hurled Mantris across the field.

Purple lightning crackled between Centipoid's fangs as it turned to Stingslash. The Darkus beast reared up, then dove into the field, disappearing. An instant later, it rose up right underneath Stingslash and gripped it with its fangs. Then it tossed Stingslash into the air like a baseball.

A portal of purple light opened up in the sky above the field, swallowing both of Tatsuya's Bakugan.

Tatsuya was in shock. "Whoa! He took both of mine out!"

"Unfortunately for your Mantris and Stingslash, there is no escape from the Darkus Power of this card," Masquerade said smugly. "Now they're headed for the Doom Dimension."

Tatsuya fell to his knees. "I'm so beat."

"Don't know how to break it to you, but your Bakugan aren't coming back — ever," Masquerade said darkly.

"You're kidding, right?" Tatsuya asked.

Masquerade grinned. "When it comes to Bakugan, I'm always deadly serious."

CHAPTER 3

A CHANCE *MEAT*-ING

Across town, Runo Misaki sat at the counter of an empty restaurant. She wore her aqua-blue hair in two ponytails. A pink pouch strapped around her waist held her Bakugan. Behind the counter, a man in an apron dried glasses with a towel. A plump woman with blue hair washed dishes in a sink behind him.

"Why do I have to work here, Daddy?" Runo complained. "Why? I hate being a waitress! It's like the most boring job in the whole world."

Runo's dad smiled warmly. "Oh, come on, Runo. Your mom and I love having you around."

"What-ever!" Runo said. "But a girl can't get rich when the place is deserted."

"I call it a midday slump," Mr. Misaki said cheerfully.

Runo's mom turned away from the sink. "You should be very proud of your family business, Runo. Why, your father is constantly bragging about you."

She motioned to the restaurant walls, which were covered with pictures of Runo. Runo as a baby. Runo in kindergarten. Runo riding her bike for the first time . . .

"Have a look around, dear. Your father has turned this place into a shrine for his little princess," she pointed out.

"Well, can't a father be proud of his only daughter?" Runo's dad asked.

Runo shook her head. "I have got the freakiest parents on the planet!"

Mrs. Misaki changed the subject. "Say Runo, seeing as we're a little slow around here, would you mind running an errand for me? Grocery Town is having a giant meat sale. If you go, just maybe I'll make you some liver kabobs!"

Runo's blue-green eyes lit up. "Oh, I adore liver kabobs!"

Soon she was marching toward Grocery Town, singing happily.

"I love liver kabobs, liver kabobs . . ."

At the same time, Dan marched into the market from the opposite direction.

"Loin tips, loin tips . . ."

The two friends marched closer to each other with every step.

"Liver kabobs, liver kabobs . . ."

"Loin tips, loin tips . . ."

SLAM!

Runo and Dan bumped into each other. They both fell backwards, landing on their butts. Their empty shopping bags went flying out of their hands.

"Runo?" Dan asked.

"Dan?" asked Runo. "Do you live around here?"

"Yeah," Dan replied. "How about you?"

"I totally do," Runo said. "Just around the corner."

Dan felt weird. It felt strange seeing Runo in person. "Well, we finally meet," he said.

Runo nodded. "Yeah, finally, after talking online for such a long time."

Dan smiled. "So we could be neighbors or something."

Runo jumped to her feet, excited. "I got an idea," she said. She took a Bakugan out of her pouch. "Let's have a battle!"

"You mean, like, right here?" Dan asked.

"No, silly," Runo answered. "How about we meet later in the park?"

Dan stood up. "Nah. I wouldn't want to take your Bakugan," he said. "I'm a pretty good brawler. Well, catch ya later."

Dan picked up his shopping bag and walked off. Runo was a little surprised. Did Dan really think he was too good to battle her?

Then she noticed something on the ground. It looked

like an orange wristwatch with a tiny screen instead of a clock face. But Runo knew what it was.

"Dan dropped his Baku-pod," Runo realized. She picked it up. A tiny red mailbox appeared on the screen.

"Welcome, Dan," Dan's Baku-pod said.

"He's got a message!" Runo said.

Masquerade's face appeared on the screen next.

"Hello, Dan," he said. "Masquerade here with a little invitation for you. Meet me at the river this afternoon at three o'clock. And come alone, if you know what's good for you!"

The screen went blank.

"I don't like that guy!" Runo fumed. "Someone's got to stop him before he ruins everything."

She clutched her fingers tightly around Dan's Baku-pod. "And that someone is going to be me!"

CHAPTER 4

RUNO'S FIRST MOVE

Dan jogged back home, his shopping bag now full of loin tips.

"I really gotta step on it. I'm late!" Dan said as he ran. "Mom's gonna be worried."

He glanced at his wrist — and for the first time, noticed his missing Baku-pod.

"Oh man!" he cried. It must have fallen off when he bumped into Runo. "I gotta go back and get it."

He raced back to the mall, but he couldn't find his Baku-pod anywhere.

"Ya gotta be kidding! Where did it do?" he wondered. He thought for a moment. "Unless Runo saw it first and snagged it . . ."

At three o'clock, Runo went to the meeting point at the river, eager to battle Masquerade. Instead, she found Tatsuya waiting for her.

"Who are you supposed to be?" Tatsuya asked.

"Name's Runo," she replied. "It looks like Masquerade sent me here to battle against you."

Tatsuya laughed. "My battle's supposed to be against a guy named Dan, not some lame girl."

"Dan's the one who's lame!" Runo replied angrily.

"You mean you beat Dan?" Tatsuya asked, his eyes wide.

"Who cares about Dan?" Runo replied. "Did you come here to battle or what, Mr. Not-So-Big Shot? I'm challenging you!" She thrust out her arm and pointed at him.

Tatsuya's brown eyes shone. "Okay, but you'll be sorry, 'cause I'm gonna beat you good!"

Tatsuya and Runo each held up a Gate Card. "Field Open!" they cried. The air around them swirled as the Bakugan field formed, blocking them from the real world.

"Hey, hang on!"

They looked up to see Dan running toward them. He jumped into the field just in time.

"Runo, what do you think you're doing?" he asked.

Runo put her hands on her hips. "Here's a better question. What do you think you're doing, following me?"

"Well, I thought you might have found my Baku-pod," Dan answered.

Runo held out Dan's Baku-pod. "Is this it?"

Dan grabbed it from her with a happy cry.

"Hey, is that the thanks I get for finding it?" Runo asked. She was trying to distract Dan — if he saw the message from Masquerade, he would know Runo had accepted the challenge in his place.

But Dan saw the message right away, and quickly read it. He turned to Tatsuya, confused.

"You're not Masquerade," he said.

Tatsuya snarled impatiently. "Hello! Waiting for a battle here."

Runo looked at Dan. "Please, I know what you're thinking, but let me battle him," she pleaded. "Masquerade set up this battle and he's the one who stole my Bakugan from me. I want to have my revenge, Dan. I want it! I know it's no big deal to you, but it's the whole world to me."

"I don't know," Dan replied. He hated to give up a battle.

Tatsuya stepped forward, angrily waving his fist. "C'mon, c'mon, let's get this show on the road already!" he said impatiently.

"Keep your shirt on. You in a mood to lose?" Dan asked.

Tatsuya stopped, surprised.

"'Cause Runo's gonna whip you big time!" Dan said, grinning.

"Really?" Runo asked.

Dan nodded. That was all Runo needed. She threw down her Gate Card.

"Gate Card open now!"

Tatsuya threw down a Gate Card too. He also tossed another card into the field — a present from Masquerade.

The Doom Card.

Okay, Runo, she told herself. *This is your chance. It's all or nothing.*

She held up her first Bakugan. "Everything rides on you, Juggernoid," she whispered. "Bakugan Brawl!"

She tossed out a Bakugan ball. It transformed into a huge beast that looked like a turtle covered in white and gold armor. Like all of Runo's Bakugan, Juggernoid was a Haos type. The creature roared as it stood on the Gate Card. It had 320 Gs — a decent amount of power.

"What do you think of my opening move?" she asked Dan.

"Not bad," Dan replied.

"Now to put the plan into action!" Runo said.

Tatsuya smirked. "Tell me you're joking. Your Bakugan's a turtle? The only thing it can do is crawl. Ha!"

"Right. I'm just a girl. What do I know about battling anyway?" Runo shot back.

Tatsuya held up an orange and red Bakugan. "Now it's my turn to play," he said, throwing out the ball. "Bakugan Brawl!"

The ball landed on the Gate Card in front of Juggernoid. Tatsuya yelled "Bakugan Stand!" and the Bakugan transformed, flying into the air. It looked like a red cocoon, but the cocoon opened to reveal an orange humanoid with red leathery wings and a face like a dinosaur. Two thick, gray horns spiraled from his forehead. The beast had 330 Gs.

"Let's do some damage!" Tatsuya yelled. "Gate Card open!"

Waves of fire flew from the Gate Card, swirling around Garganoid.

"Garganoid Power Level 430 Gs," Dan's Baku-pod reported.

Garganoid screeched and a blast of fire shot from its mouth, aimed right at Juggernoid.

"Okay, my turn," Runo said. "Ability Card Lightning Shield Activate!"

A glowing bubble of light appeared around Juggernoid like a shield.

"Garganoid Power decrease 100 Gs," Dan's Baku-pod said.

But the fiery blast dissolved the Lightning Shield, leaving Juggernoid open to attack. Garganoid flew across the field, slamming into Juggernoid. The Bakugan flew into the air — and then got sucked right into the Doom Dimension!

"How'd he do that?" Runo wondered.

"No clue," Dan answered. "His Bakugan was only 10 Gs stronger than yours!"

Runo gasped. *This is not looking good for me,* she realized. *I've got to stop this losing streak before I lose all my Bakugan!*

Hey, Runo, are you okay?" Dan asked.

Runo shook off her worried thoughts. She had a battle to win.

And now she had a plan.

"Bakugan Brawl!" she cried. She tossed a Bakugan onto the field, and it landed on the Gate Card in front of her.

"Bakugan Stand!"

With a roar, the Bakugan transformed into a Haos Saurus, a muscled, armored beast that stood on two legs. Saurus had a dinosaur-like face with five sharp horns protruding from different points on his head.

Only two left, Runo thought. *Gotta make this work!*

Tatsuya pointed at Saurus and laughed.

"You kill me! You really think you stand a chance?" he asked. "Or do you want to pack it in?"

Runo grunted in frustration. She was pretty tired of Tatsuya's trash talking.

Her Tigrerra floated up in front of her face.

"Let me finish this," Tigrerra said.

"No," Runo replied. "This is my battle. I have a great strategy worked out. Just wait!"

Tigrerra nodded. "As you wish."

"You sure about this, Runo?" Dan asked. He knew Tigrerra had a lot of G power — maybe enough to take down Garganoid.

"Trust me, Dan, I've got this totally under control," she said firmly. "It's true I haven't been the best brawler in the past, but I know I can read this guy. You gave me a chance, now let me prove myself."

Tatsuya snickered. "Your little love fest is making me sick! Bakugan Brawl!"

He hurled out Garganoid once more. The Bakugan let out a piercing screech as he unfurled his powerful wings. Garganoid stood on the Gate Card facing Saurus.

Tatsuya threw out a card.

"Ability Card activate. Fire Judge!"

Flames leapt from the card, surrounding Garganoid. The beast absorbed them, his body glowing hot with fiery power.

"Garganoid Power Increase to 430 Gs," reported Dan's Baku-pod. *"Saurus remains stable with 290 Gs."*

Dan wondered what Runo was up to. That power boost didn't look good for Saurus at all!

"I'm down to my last chance to win," Runo said. "Ability Counter Activate!"

Runo threw out the card, and the burning energy drained out of Garganoid.

"*Counter Attack neutralizes Garganoid Power Increase,*" said Dan's Baku-pod. Garganoid's power dropped back down to 330 Gs.

"Nice try!" Tatsuya said sarcastically. His Bakugan still had more Gs than Saurus.

"He's right, Runo," Dan agreed. "That wasn't much of a move. His Garganoid's got power — and loads of it!"

"Utilize me!" Tigrerra urged.

But Runo smiled calmly. "No. I can do this!"

Dan was surprised. What was Runo planning?

"Okay, let's get this over with!" Tatsuya called out impatiently. "Garganoid attack!"

Garganoid screeched and flew across the field.

"Just like I thought!" Runo said. "Saurus . . . Gate Card Open!"

The Gate Card flipped over, and Saurus began to glow with white light.

She turned to Dan. "Okay, watch and learn. With this card, Saurus's power level will increase to the same level as my strongest Tigrerra!"

Saurus's Gs quickly climbed from 290 to 340.

"No way!" Tatsuya yelled in shock.

"Yeah, come and get it!" Runo taunted.

Bam! Saurus socked Garganoid with a powerful punch. Garganoid transformed back into a Bakugan ball and rolled at Tatsuya's feet.

"I win!" Runo cheered.

"Settle down!" Dan told her. "You just won one round. You didn't win the whole battle."

"I'm just getting started," Runo promised. She threw down another Gate Card. "Bakugan Brawl!"

Runo threw Saurus onto the Gate Card.

"You only get once chance at being lucky, girl," Tatsuya said. "Bakugan Brawl!"

He tossed out a Pyrus beast with the head of a lion, the body of a dragon, and a snake for a tail. Griffon stood on the Gate Card and snarled, showing a mouth full of sharp teeth.

"Ability Card Activate!" Tatsuya said. "Fire Wall!"

Waves of fire poured from the card, surrounding Griffon.

"Too bad you don't know how to fight fire with fire, 'cause my Fire Wall's gonna drop your Power Level by over 50 Gs," Tatsuya said.

Dan was impressed. "Man, he's good, for real."

Then Runo turned over her Gate Card. "Supernova, activate!"

Saurus began to pulsate with white light.

"Sensing power level change," Dan's Baku-pod said.

The two Bakugan switched G power levels — now Saurus had 360 Gs, and Griffon had 240.

"No!" Tatsuya cried.

Pow! Saurus punched Griffon, and the Bakugan transformed back into a ball.

Runo grinned. "How does it feel to lose to a girl?" she called out. "Huh, tough guy? I just pulled the old power switch-a-roo on you and it worked to perfection."

"That was awesome!" Dan said. "How'd you figure out his counter move?"

"It was easy," Runo said sweetly. "He battles like you so he's quite predictable."

She turned back to the field and threw out a new Gate Card. Then she held up Saurus once more.

"Okay, Saurus, it's up to you," she said softly. She tossed him onto the field. "Bakugan Brawl!"

Saurus stood on the Gate Card.

"That's it! You're going down!" Tatsuya cried angrily. He threw out a red and orange ball. "Bakugan Brawl! Bakugan Stand!"

The ball opened up, transforming into a frightening humanoid beast. His body was covered with sharp red armor. His powerful arms ended in long, sharp claws. Gold blades jutted out from his shoulders. His face was a creepy mask of teeth and glowing blue eyes.

"Do your worst, Fear Ripper!" Tatsuya yelled. "Show no mercy and rip her Saurus apart!"

CHAPTER 6

RUNO'S STRATEGY

Before Fear Ripper could attack, Runo held up her hand.

"Gate Card Open! Activate Now!" she yelled.

A wall of rainbow light appeared between Saurus and Fear Ripper. The Pyrus Bakugan lashed out with his claws, but they couldn't break the rainbow barrier.

"What are you doing? You're not battling!" Tatsuya cried out in frustration.

"That's right! I don't have to," Runo replied. "I'm tired of losing my Bakugan! This is supposed to be a game. Right, Tigrerra?"

The Bakugan floated into Runo's hand. "You humans are full of surprises."

Runo smiled at Tigrerra. "I've been saving the best for last," she whispered. "I figure with your power, we can finish off his Fear Ripper and walk away with a win!"

"Your wish is my command," Tigrerra replied.

"We can't afford to lose this one, Tigrerra," Runo went on. "It's all or nothing. Saurus is waiting for you."

"I'm impressed by your patience, human," Tigrerra replied. "By my calculations, your strategy may yet be successful."

Runo grinned. "Hey, I appreciate the vote of confidence!"

"You can rely on me to defeat Fear Ripper," Tigrerra said confidently. "Let's get this over with, shall we?"

Runo nodded. "Bakugan Brawl!"

She threw out Tigrerra, who stood on the Gate Card next to Taurus. In her full form, Tigrerra was a powerful Haos beast with sharp claws and gold spikes down her back.

"Let's brawl!" Runo and Tatsuya yelled.

Fear Ripper flew at Saurus, his long claws extended. *Slam!* He knocked Saurus down on his back.

Tigrerra looked at Fear Ripper and growled. "You're mine!"

She jumped at Fear Ripper, and the Pyrus Bakugan swiped at her. She leaped out of the way and landed on her feet next to Saurus.

"Are you ready, Saurus?" she asked.

"Never more!" Saurus roared back. He stood up and aimed a punch at Fear Ripper. The Bakugan held back Saurus's blows with his claws.

Saurus turned to Tigrerra. "Springboard, now!"

She ran across the field and pounced onto Saurus's back. Then she leaped higher, her claws extended.

"Ability Card Activate! Crystal Fang!" Runo yelled.

Tigrerra glowed with extra power as the Ability Card took effect. She lashed out at Fear Ripper with her claws. The Bakugan turned back into a ball and rolled back to Tatsuya.

"How'd she —" Tatsuya wondered.

"Fear Ripper eliminated."

"That was sweet!" Dan said. "I've never seen team-work like that before!"

The Bakugan field vanished around them. Tatsuya left without a word. Runo and Dan leaned back against the green grass, enjoying the river breeze.

"Not bad, Runo. You sure showed him," Dan said.

"I appreciate it, Dan," Runo replied. "I tried my best."

"Excuse me, human, but I too must say how impressed I was," said Tigrerra, who sat in Runo's hand. "Congratulations."

Runo sat up. "You're sweet, Tigrerra."

"Your patience and skill surpassed anything I have ever witnessed before," Tigrerra went on.

"Wow! Coming from you, I am totally honored!" Runo said, her aqua eyes shining. "But you do realize it was you and Saurus who did the dirty work. Oh, and if you don't mind me saying, you were kind of cute back there."

Tigrerra's face turned pink. "No, I don't mind."

"Hey, look, she's blushing!" Dan said, pointing.

Later that day, Runo and Dan's families got together at the beach.

"It looks like Dan and Runo are getting along," Dan's mom told Mr. and Mrs. Misaki. "I'm glad you both could join us out here for our little beach barbecue."

"So honey, do you think there's any of your world-famous loin tips left?" asked Dan's dad.

Dan and Runo stood over by the grill. Dan pointed his chopsticks at Runo.

"Quit hogging!" he cried.

"Me hogging? You practically ate everything!" Runo replied.

"Nobody comes between me and my loin tips, got it?" Dan said.

"I didn't touch your stupid loin tips, beef breath!" Runo shot back.

Tigrerra and Drago watched them both.

"Just when you think you've got them all figured out . . ." Tigrerra sighed.

Drago nodded. "Tigrerra, my friend, I don't think we'll *ever* understand these humans!"

CHAPTER 7

A SURPRISING CHALLENGE

Don't be a wimp, Runo," Dan complained. "Let's do Extreme Mountain next."

"I want to ride the Ferris wheel!" Runo said.

It was a week later, and Dan and Runo decided to go to the amusement park together. But what started out as a fun time was turning into a huge argument. The two friends faced each other under the shadow of a large Ferris wheel. Behind them, crowds lined up to ride a spiraling roller coaster.

"Extreme Mountain!" Dan cried.

"Ferris wheel!" Runo shot back.

Dan rolled his eyes. "Oh, whoopee! A big wheel that goes round and round. What a blast!"

"Just because it doesn't go up and down at a hundred miles an hour doesn't mean it won't be fun," Runo pointed out.

"Yeah, it'll be boring," Dan said.

Runo reached into her pocket. "Well, I've still got six tickets. How many do you have left?"

Dan's eyes grew wide. He didn't have any tickets left, and he had a horrible feeling that he knew what Runo was about to say. "No, you wouldn't!" he begged.

Runo turned her back to him. "I guess you shouldn't have wasted your money on all those gnarly corndogs. I'll share my tickets if we go on the Ferris wheel first."

"You are so brutal!" Dan yelled in frustration. "I knew this would turn into a snooze fest!"

Runo shrugged. "You spent your whole allowance. You've been stuffing your face with junk food all day. You've got no money left. If you want to get on Extreme Mountain, you'd better be nice to me."

"I bought you a corndog. Isn't that worth something?" Dan asked.

This just made Runo angry. "A corndog?" she shrieked. "Listen up, buddy. We're going on the Ferris wheel next. If you want my ticket, do as I say!"

"Ten kids have already lost their lunch on Extreme Mountain today, so that tells you how awesome it is," Dan said. "What more do you want? That's where we're going!"

"You can't slow down for one minute! That's why you never know what's going on around you," Runo said, her face bright red. "Do you even know where you are? You are such a *lost* loser!"

Drago poked his head out of the pouch Dan kept him in. "There they go again," he said.

Tigrerra peeked out of her pouch. "These humans are indeed a curious species," she remarked.

"Extreme Mountain!"

"Ferris Wheel!"

Yay! Woohoo! All right!

Luckily, the sound of cheering distracted Dan and Runo. They saw a large crowd gathered in front of a stage. They walked over to see two boys dressed in blue tuxedos. The boys looked alike, with big gray eyes and smooth, shoulder-length hair. But one boy had purple hair, and the other had red hair.

The purple-haired boy reached into a hat and pulled out a bunch of flowers that rained over the stage. Then the flowers vanished into thin air.

"Awesome!" Dan cried.

"Yeah, cool," Runo agreed.

"Ladies and gents, can we have two volunteers for our next illusion?" asked the red-haired boy.

Dan and Runo frantically waved their hands. "Yeah, pick us! Pick us!" they yelled.

The boy pointed at them. "You two — come on up here!

"Oh yeah!" Dan and Runo called out.

They walked up onstage as the magicians wheeled out a small table with a white tablecloth. A deck of cards sat on the cloth.

"We'll start with a card trick," said the red-haired boy. He fanned the cards out on the table. "Pick a card, any card."

Dan stroked his chin. "Hmm. Which one should I choose?"

"Dan, pick a card!" Runo said impatiently.

"Chill, I'm thinking," he said. Then he reached out and grabbed one. "I pick this card here."

Dan looked at the card and gasped. The card showed the face of a frightening beast on a black background.

"A Doom Card!" Runo cried.

Dan couldn't believe it. "That's twisted!"

"Yeah, and you know why? Masquerade's behind this," Runo guessed.

"You're right," said the red-haired boy. "Let me introduce myself and my brother. I'm Kenta."

"And I'm Kenji," said the purple-haired boy.

"Runo, right?" Kenta said. "And you must be Dan Kuso. Masquerade says you're the one to beat."

"You up for a battle?" Kenji asked.

"Always," Dan said.

"Yeah, Dan, I can handle these two," Runo said.

"What?" Dan replied, confused.

"This is all a setup by Masquerade," Runo explained. "He's watching you and if you take part in this battle you'll be playing right into his hands."

"Yeah, maybe," Dan said. "But so what? I can't back out of this."

"You have to!" Runo pleaded.

"They challenged me, not you," Dan pointed out.

The crowd for the magic show was starting to get restless. Kenta eyed Dan and Runo with a sinister grin.

"You two up for a combination battle?"

CHAPTER 8

KENJI'S MOVE: MARIONETTE

combination battle?" Runo asked.

"The two of you against the two of us," Kenji explained. "That way the odds are even. That sounds fair, doesn't it?"

"Sure! Let's do it!" Dan replied eagerly. "Ready when you are!"

Dan, Runo, Kenji and Kenta each held up a Gate Card. The air began to glow and swirl as the Bakugan field formed around them.

"Bakugan Field Open!" they yelled.

The noise and chatter from the amusement park faded around them. Kenta and Kenji each held up a card.

"Doom Card set!" the two boys said at once.

The Doom Cards sank into the field, and the sky overhead turned black. The gateway to the Doom Dimension had formed.

Then the four brawlers threw out their Gate Cards.

"Gate Card set!"

The four cards fell to create a square field between the two teams of brawlers. Kenta made the first move. He opened his hand to reveal a Pyrus Bakugan. Then he placed the ball in a special holder he wore on his wrist. He extended his arm, and the ball went flying onto the field.

"Bakugan Stand!"

The Bakugan transformed into a Robotallian, a tall robot-like creature with a shiny red metal body. His huge fists and large feet were gold, and two red shields covered the Bakugan's arms. Blue eyes glowed from his smooth metal face.

Kenta followed up with another card. "Ability Activate. Robotallian Enforcement!"

Robotallian began to glow with red heat as the card charged him up with extra energy.

Power level 380 Gs," Dan's Baku-pod reported.

"Ha! What a bonehead maneuver. He's using a fire attribute just like me," Dan pointed out. He reached for his Bakugan.

"Wait, Dan!" Runo warned. "What if it's some kind of trap?"

Dan paused. "A trap?"

"Get with the program," Runo replied. "Haven't you learned anything from Drago?"

"Yeah, I sure have," Dan said. "Look, I know that if I

sent my Griffon in he's got the skills to go one-on-one with his Robotallian."

Dan reached into his pocket and took out his Griffon. "Bakugan Brawl!" he cried, hurling it out onto the field.

Griffon rolled onto a Gate Card behind Robotallian. "Bakugan Stand!"

Griffon transformed into his true form and roared, shaking his shaggy mane.

"You're up, Kenji," Kenta said. "Now go!"

Kenji nodded. He used a wrist device to toss a purple and black Bakugan ball onto the field. The Bakugan stood on a card to the right of Griffon. Then it transformed into a Darkus Mantris.

Kenji held up another card. "Ability Activate! Marionette!"

Jagged streaks of purple light came out of Mantris's front claws. The light gripped Griffon, pulling the Bakugan across the field and leaving him on the card right in front of Robotallian.

"Check it out, brother!" Kenji called out. "The Marionette is an ability card that lets you move any standing Bakugan to any part of the battlefield you want!"

Dan watched, stunned. There was nothing he could do to help Griffon now.

Bam! Robotallian slammed Griffon with a powerful punch. Dan's Bakugan flew up into the air, and then got sucked into the Doom Dimension.

"No, Griffin!" Dan cried.

Robotallian turned back into a Bakugan ball and Kenta caught him with one hand.

"You should put your Bakugans in show business," he teased. "They do a great vanishing act!"

CHAPTER 9

MORE TRICKS

That was some mean hocus-pocus," Dan said, shaken. "What's next, is he gonna pull a rabbit out of his hat?"

"That was just one of their cards, and it cost you a Bakugan!" Runo said crossly. "Who knows what else they might have up their sleeves?"

Dan frowned. "Thanks! You're a big help."

Drago and Tigrerra floated up between the fighting friends.

"Remain calm," Drago urged. "Utilize the Bakugans you have. You can do this."

"Make your move, my lady," Tigrerra told Runo.

Runo looked thoughtful. "His Mantris is tough but he's got to have a weak spot somewhere," she said, checking her Baku-pod. "His power level is at 350. And I'm pretty sure that Gate Card can boost the power of Darkus. That's just the kind of juice I need."

She held up a yellow and white Bakugan ball. "There's only one way to find out. Bakugan Brawl!"

She tossed out her Serpenoid. The Bakugan stood on the card in front of Mantris and hissed.

"Ability Activate! Combination of Haos and Darkus!"

Serpenoid uncoiled, towering over Mantris. Runo grinned.

"A light-attributed Bakugan can spike its power level by a hundred Gs against a Darkus Bakugan," she said proudly.

"Calculating Serpenoid power level at 400 Gs," said Dan's Baku-pod.

"That won't help you!" Kenta sneered. "I'll show you why. Gate Card open!"

The card underneath the Bakugan flipped over.

"Level down!" Kenji yelled.

Serpenoid roared as the extra power drained from its body.

"Adjusting power level . . . 300 Gs."

"The 'level down' command card can forcibly decrease the power level by 100 Gs once your Bakugan level goes over 400," Kenta explained. "You wasted the combination of Darkus and Haos and now you'll pay!"

Kenji thrust out his arm. "Mantris! Send him off the field!"

Mantris lunged at Serpenoid, striking the Haos beast with a sharp claw.

Bam! Mantris knocked Serpenoid backward. A purple vortex opened up in the black sky overhead, sucking Serpenoid into the Doom Dimension.

"No! Snakie! Come back!" Runo yelled.

"Smooth move, Runo. You really know how to dish it out," Dan said sarcastically. "That's what you call a trap!"

"Well, you should know!" Runo shot back.

"Stop it, you two," Drago scolded.

"Your fight belongs on the battlefield, not here," Tigrerra reminded them.

Runo and Dan grunted and turned away from each other, arms folded.

"Stop this!" Tigrerra urged.

Across the field, Kenta and Kenji were ready to finish the fight.

"Gate Card, set!" Kenta yelled, throwing out a new card. He followed up by throwing out Robotallian again. "Bakugan Stand!"

Robotallian grunted as he got into fighting stance.

"Oh, no you don't!" Dan cried, throwing out another card. Then he tossed out a Pyrus Bakugan. "Bakugan Brawl!"

His Saurus landed on a card next to Robotallian and stood, transforming into his true form.

"Saurus power level is 290 Gs," reported Dan's Baku-pod.

"You're taking a chance," Kenta said, grinning. "You sure you want to risk it?"

"You know it!" Dan said confidently. He held up a card. "Go!"

Fire began to swirl around Saurus's body. He opened his mouth, and a stream of hot flame shot out.

"You are gonna get played now, magic man," Dan explained. "That was the 'power charge' ability card and it just zapped Saurus's power level by a hundred Gs. In the next battle he can attack anywhere on the field!"

"Wow, slammin' move," Runo said. "You thought of that all by yourself?"

"Hey, watch it," Dan warned.

It was Kenta's move now. "Bakugan Brawl!"

He tossed out a ball, and a purple and black Centipoid stood on the card facing Saurus. Then he held up a card.

"Ability Card activate. Pyrus versus Darkus!"

Runo looked worried. "I've never heard of that before."

"It's another combination ability card," Dan said. "Don't sweat it. It won't do much good against Saurus's jungle breath!"

Saurus breathed out a stream of flame.

"Adjusting power levels. Saurus at 390 Gs," said Dan's Baku-pod.

"Turn up the heat, Saurus," Dan yelled. "Gate Card open!"

The Gate Card underneath Saurus flipped over, and he began to glow with a new power surge.

"That'll pump us up another 50 Gs," Dan said proudly.

"Adjusting Saurus power level . . . 440 Gs."

"Now squash that bug!" Dan commanded.

Saurus stomped across the card — but Centipoid wrapped its long body around Saurus, stopping him.

"Hey, what gives?" Dan cried. "Saurus has got way more juice than that creepy crawler!"

"Oh no! Centipoid's power is spiking!" Runo said.

"Adjusting Centipoid's power level . . . stabilizing at 460 Gs."

Kenta chuckled. "Pyrus and Darkus are opposites. When I use them together on a fire-attributed Bakugan like yours, it pushes my power level up 100 Gs. Combined they can be a powerful force. It's all in the cards!"

"That's what I call a combination battle," added Kenji.

"You said it brother!" Kenta agreed.

Kenji scowled at Dan. "Your Bakugan's time is up. Centipoid, finish him!"

"No, Saurus!" Dan yelled.

But there was nothing he could do. Centipoid squeezed Saurus tightly as the Doom Dimension opened up above him. Saurus roared and struggled, but the powerful energy pulled him up. Then he disappeared.

"Saurus! Come back!" Dan cried.

# CHAPTER 10

ONE PLUS ONE EQUALS
SWEET MOVES!

an, you can't win!" Kenta taunted him. "You've got one Bakugan left."

Dan shook his head. "Darn! I can't take another knock out," he muttered. "We need to scheme something real big."

Runo's eyes sparkled. "I know!" She held up a card. "This should do the trick!"

She threw out the card. "Gate Card set!"

Then she tossed out a yellow and white Bakugan ball. It stood on the new card and transformed into a Haos Saurus.

"Haos Saurus recognized," said Dan's Baku-pod. *"Calculating power level at 290 Gs."*

Kenta grinned and hurled out another Pyrus Bakugan. It landed on the same card as Saurus.

"Bakugan Stand!" The ball transformed into a creature that looked like a medieval knight in red armor. A long cape hung down his back, and two red shields curved up from his shoulders. He held the handle of a sword in his hand, but the sword had no blade.

"Wait, Kenta!" Kenji warned.

"Don't worry, brother," Kenta said confidently. He held up a card. "Ability Card activate! Siege, take it. Fire Sword!"

A blade made of flame sprung from the sword handle.

"Go, Siege, battle! Finish them!" Kenta cried.

Siege growled and moved to attack Saurus. But Runo just smiled.

"I knew you were gonna do that," she said.

Kenta, Kenji, and even Dan were surprised.

"What?" Dan asked.

"All right! Gate Card open!" Runo yelled. "Triple Battle Activate!"

Siege tried to swing his sword, but the Gate Card flipped over before he could move. Runo turned to Dan.

"Now to get this fight really kickin' we need a third Bakugan on the battlefield," she said. "Dan, if you're good to go, we need you!"

Dan nodded. "All right! I see where you're coming from. With two Bakugans we can pull off some sweet moves."

"Yeah!" Runo cheered.

Dan took Drago from his pocket. "Wicked! Let's slam 'em!" he said. "Right, Drago? Bakugan Brawl!"

Dan threw out Drago, who landed on the card next to Saurus. A Pyrus Dragonoid, Drago had a scaly red body with yellow scales, huge red wings, and clawed feet. He let out a roar, happy to be free.

"Battle!" Dan yelled.

Saurus moved first. He punched Siege, sending the knight hurling backwards.

"Siege! Above you!" Kenta yelled.

Puzzled, Siege raised his head to see Drago flying above him.

"Ability Card activate. Boosted Dragon!" Dan yelled.

A huge fireball exploded from Drago's mouth. It engulfed Siege, covering him in flames. Drago turned back into a Bakugan ball and bounced back into Dan's hand.

"We did it, Dan!" Runo said.

"Congratulations," said Tigrerra. "That was an excellent strategy, my lady."

"Well done," Drago agreed. "You caught your opponents off guard."

Across the field, Kenta was stunned.

"What? My Siege . . ."

"You had your chance, brother," Kenji told him. "Now

it's my turn. With this card I'll take control of the battle. Gate Card set!"

He threw out another card and then followed with a Bakugan ball.

"Bakugan Stand!"

The ball landed on a Gate Card and transformed into a sinister-looking Bakugan with a humanoid body topped with striped black and purple horns. The creature had jagged purple wings and held a large, sharp scythe in one hand.

Dan gasped. "The Reaper!"

CHAPTER 11

TIGRERRA TEAMS UP

Dan and Runo had both seen this Bakugan before — when they faced Masquerade.

"Uh, Dan, you take ugly," Runo said. She nodded toward Kenta's Robotallian, who stood on the field. "I'll deal with the other one."

She tossed out her Haos Saurus. "Bakugan Brawl!"

Saurus stood on a Gate Card next to Robotallian's card. "Shade Ability Activate!" Runo yelled.

A light storm began to crackle on the field. Robotallian growled as he felt his power being sapped.

"Adjusting Robotallian power level . . . 330 Gs."

Runo smiled. "'Shade Ability' is one of the choicest cards," she said, pleased. "It can squash the other ability card effects that are happening on the field!"

Kenta scowled. "They've got us again!"

"Wait, Kenta," Kenji warned.

But Kenta was furious. "No, Kenji! I'm the one who

taught you how to play Bakugan. I know the game way better than you do! Bakugan Brawl!"

Without waiting for his brother's advice, Kenta hurled a Pyrus Bakugan onto the field. It landed on the same card as Saurus. It transformed into Garganoid, who unfurled his red wings as he stood on the card.

"Gate Card Open!" Runo yelled. She needed to give Saurus a quick power boost.

But Kenta had other plans.

"This is it. Ability Card activate!" he yelled. "Backfire!"

A wave of flame washed over the field, and the glowing light around Saurus began to fade.

"Power level drop detected," said Dan's Baku-pod. *"Adjusting level. Haos Saurus now at 290 Gs."*

Kenta grinned. "Garganoid, attack!"

But Runo was ready for him. "Come and get it. Ability Card activate. Cut-in-Saber!"

As Runo held up the card, Tigrerra pounced onto the field. She landed next to Saurus and roared, ready to battle.

"What is she doing?" Kenta asked.

"You can thank the Cut-in-Saber Ability Card for that," Runo answered coolly. "Time to clean house. Go!"

Saurus and Tigrerra charged at Garganoid.

Bam!

Slam!

They quickly took down Garganoid, who disappeared from the field. Tigrerra bounced back into Runo's hand.

"Thanks, Tigrerra," Runo said. "You sent that big bad Garganoid packing!"

"That's nothing," Dan said boastfully. "Hey, Drago, you fighting machine. Turn it on!"

He tossed Drago onto the field, and he rolled right in front of Reaper.

"Yeah, right onto Reaper's orb card!" Dan cheered. "Bakugan Stand!"

Drago transformed, flapping his large wings.

"He's no match for the Reaper," Kenji taunted. "Gate Card open!"

The card flipped over and Reaper began to glow with purple light as the card's power gave him an extra charge.

"So we meet again, Drago," he said.

"Traitor!" Drago replied. "I'll make you pay for your betrayal!"

Drago knew that Masquerade wanted to destroy Vestroia, the home world of the Bakugan. And Reaper worked for Masquerade.

"Let's brawl!" Dan and Kenji yelled at the same time.

Reaper reached out to punch Drago, but Drago grabbed his hands in his claws, holding him back.

"Masquerade has got you fooled, Reaper," Drago said, grunting with the effort of fighting off his opponent. "You're only being used!"

"What do you know?" Reaper replied. "Masquerade gives me everything I want. If I have to destroy my own kind, then so be it! And you're next on my list, Drago!"

The purple light glowed brighter, and Reaper growled. "Oh, I can taste the power!"

"Power level . . . 420 Gs."

"I . . . will . . . stop . . . you," Drago said, straining to fight back.

"Take him down!" Kenta ordered.

Drago reared back his head. "Boosted Dragon!"

Whoosh! A river of flame flowed from Drago's mouth, striking Reaper and forcing him back.

"Yeah, that's it!" Dan cheered.

"Take that demon to school, Drago!" Runo yelled.

Kenji frowned and threw out a card. "Gate Card set!"

He threw out his Pyrus Mantris again. The big bug stood on the card to the right of Robotallian.

"Mantris's power level is 350 Gs," she said. "My next Bakugan will have to be choice! I'd better use one with a pumped-up power level."

She held up her arm to throw a Bakugan, but Dan grabbed her arm, stopping her.

"Runo, hold on!"

CHAPTER 12

ONE MORE CARD UP HIS SLEEVE

hat gives?" Runo asked.

"It's weird," Dan said. "Kenji's Centipoid has a power level of 360. And the power of Mantris is 350 . . ." It didn't make sense. Why wouldn't Kenji put up a more powerful Bakugan?

Runo realized what Dan was thinking. "They must be trying to fake us out with the Gate Card!"

"Yeah," Dan agreed. "That's why Kenji put Mantris in."

Dan tried to think of a plan. "All right . . . we'll need an Ability Card. Runo, you're up! Put Saurus in the game. You first, then me."

"Gotcha!" Runo said. She tossed out a card. "Gate Card set!"

She threw out Saurus, and her aim was perfect. He landed right on the new Gate Card.

"Bakugan Stand!"

Saurus transformed and stood, waiting to battle.

Dan threw out a card next. Then he hurled Drago onto the field, aiming for the card Robotallian stood on.

"Go Drago!" Dan yelled.

"Boosted Dragon!" Drago roared. He wiped out Robotallian with one blast of his fiery dragon breath.

"Robotallian eliminated."

Kenta cried out in shock. All three of his Bakugan had been defeated! He was out of the battle.

"It's over!" he wailed.

"Done like dinner," Dan said, pleased.

No, we're still in this, Kenji told himself. *I have a Command Card. All I need to do now is get rid of Saurus with my next shot!*

"Bakugan Brawl!" Kenji yelled, throwing out another Pyrus ball. It landed on the same card as Saurus and transformed into his purple and black Centipoid.

Dan smiled slyly. "Busted," he said.

Kenji looked shocked.

"Of all the cards left to play, you had to roll up onto that one," Dan said. "You're a scammer. Your tricks don't work on us anymore."

"Okay, let me guess what that card is," Runo said, nodding to the card Mantris stood on. "The Quartet Battle card, maybe?"

Kenta's mouth opened as wide as his purple-haired brother's. How did Dan and Runo figure out their plan?

"The Quartet Battle card starts a four-way battle. Each team has to throw in one more Bakugan once the battle starts," Dan said. "You were going to use your Ability Cards to increase Mantris's power and have Centipoid there for backup, weren't you, smiley? Drago and Tigrerra would have been toast if it worked. You were going to give them a one-way ticket to the Doom Dimension! Admit it!"

"How did you know?" Kenji asked.

"Because you were so stoked for a combination battle with us!" Runo replied. "We knew you had a Quartet Battle card."

"You still won't win this battle!" Kenji called out.

Runo ignored him. "Gate Card Open! Quartet Battle!"

The card underneath Centipoid and Saurus flipped over to reveal a Quartet Battle card. Runo had thrown it out earlier. It was time to turn the tables on the brawling brothers.

Dan tossed out Drago, who joined Saurus for the battle. Drago blasted Centipoid with his powerful dragon fire. The Bakugan disappeared from the field.

"We got 'em!" Dan cheered.

"All we have to do now is deal with Mantris," Runo said. "That's one down, one to go!"

But Kenji started to chuckle.

"Hey pal, what's so funny?" Runo asked.

"It's a little early for a victory party," Kenji sneered. "I actually do have a card up my sleeve. And guess what, it's an Ability Card!"

"Which one is it?" Dan asked, worried.

Kenji threw out the card. "Ability Card activate. Twin Machetes!"

Mantris screeched as its two front legs grew longer and sharper, becoming two curved blades.

"*Mantris power level increase . . . 450 Gs,*" said Dan's Baku-pod.

"Dan! The Boosted Dragon only gives us 440 Gs. We can't beat him!" Runo exclaimed.

"No," Dan said. "It might look messed up, but it's not! If the Quartet Battle card is activated, everything will be cool. We'll be back on top after that."

"But what if it doesn't activate?" Runo asked, worried.

Dan took a deep breath. "Then Drago goes to the Doom Dimension!"

Drago floated in front of Dan's face.

"Your concern is appreciated, but this battle is too important to lose," Drago said calmly.

"What do you mean by that?" Dan asked.

"I can't explain right now, but if you have to let me go, then don't hesitate," Drago replied. "When the time comes you will know what to do. Trust yourself and trust me!"

"Drago, I trust you," Dan said softly. "You know that. Now let's do what we have to do!"

There were only two Gate Cards left on the field. Runo threw Saurus onto the empty card.

"Bakugan Brawl!"

Dan tossed Drago onto Mantris's card. "Bakugan Stand!"

"Battle!" Kenji yelled.

Mantris lashed out at Drago with his machete-sharp

claws. Drago cried out as the shining blades made contact.

"Drago, hang in there!" Dan called out.

Kenji laughed. "Your Bakugan puts up a good fight but it won't do any good. Mantris still has the higher power level. See for yourself."

Dan checked the stats on his Baku-pod, but he already knew what he'd find. Mantris had 450 Gs to Drago's 440 Gs. Drago couldn't win — without some help.

Slash! Mantris sliced at Drago's right wing. The Pyrus Bakugan fell over, his head hitting the field.

Don't worry about me, Drago had said. But Dan couldn't help it. He didn't want to lose Drago because of some annoying magician who was friends with Masquerade.

"Drago, hold on!" Dan called out.

"It's time! Mantris!" Kenji yelled. "Send him to the Doom Dimension!"

"Noooooo!" Dan wailed.

Mantris bore down on Drago.

"Are you ready, Dan?" Drago asked, his voice weak. "You know what to do."

Then his voice got stronger. "The time has come. This battle is ours!"

Drago flew up and faced Mantris. The Darkus beast roared angrily.

"Quartet Battle! Activate!" Runo and Dan yelled together.

The Gate Card Mantris and Drago stood on flipped over. Runo and Dan had used Kenji's own card against him!

"I don't believe it," Kenji said, his face turning pale. "You tricked me!"

Runo's Tigrerra jumped onto the field and landed next to Drago.

"Not two against one!" Kenji cried.

Tigrerra and Drago charged forward, ready to take down Mantris.

Slam! The Pyrus beast fell.

The battle was over. The Bakugan field disappeared around them.

"It's over now. We lost," said Kenta and Kenji. They picked up the white tablecloth and tossed it over themselves. Then they vanished into thin air.

The crowd clapped politely. Dan and Runo looked at Drago and Tigrerra, who sat in the palm of their hand.

"We did it Drago," Dan said.

"Yeah, we won!" Runo told Tigrerra.

"Cheers to a well-timed attack!" Tigrerra said.

"And a strong team," Drago added.

Runo and Dan walked off of the stage. The day was warm and bright, and Runo still had six ride tickets left.

"That battle was intense," Dan remarked. "What do you say we chill out for awhile on one of these rides? Your pick!"

"Okay!" Runo said happily.

"So let me guess," Dan began. "The Ferris wheel?"

"Are you still stoked about Extreme Mountain?" Runo asked.

Dan shrugged. "I can go on that next time. Right now I feel like kickin' back on that big old Ferris wheel."

"Not me. I'm in the mood for Extreme Mountain!" Runo said, her aqua eyes shining.

"No way," Dan replied. "We can do that next time. Let's go to the Ferris wheel."

"Extreme Mountain!" Runo said.

"Ferris wheel!" Dan shot back.

Drago and Tigrerra watched them argue.

"Ah, I suppose this was bound to happen," Drago sighed.

Tigrerra shook her head. "I'll never understand these humans!"

BAKUGAN WORLDS AND CLASSES

Each Bakugan is associated with a different world in Vestroia. Then they can be divided into different classes. Each Bakugan you own will be a combination of these two.

In these pages you'll learn about the six worlds of Vestroia, and some of the main classes of Bakugan. There are lots more to be discovered!

WORLD:
PYRUS

Pyrus Bakugan get their power from the energy of fire, which makes them intense and sometimes unpredictable. They have been known to attack using fireballs or hot streams of fiery breath

DAN'S DRAGO IS A PYRUS BAKUGAN.

WORLD:
AQUOS

Bakugan that get power from the watery world of Aquos keep their cool when things get tough. But even though they may act calm, they can unleash a tidal wave of terror on their opponents.

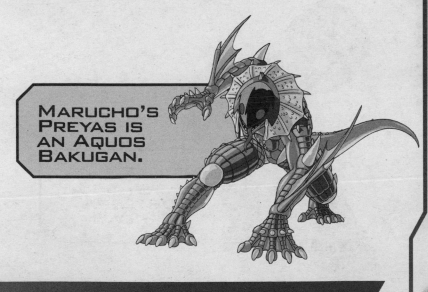

MARUCHO'S PREYAS IS AN AQUOS BAKUGAN.

WORLD:
SUBTERRA

These earthy Bakugan are masters of combat above ground — but their real strength shows when they take the brawl underground. Subterra Bakugan don't mind getting down and dirty!

JULIE'S GOREM IS A SUBTERRA BAKUGAN.

WORLD:
HAOS

Light and energy provide the power for Haos Bakugan, which make them shining stars on the field. They can blind an opponent with powerful rays.

RUNO'S TIGRERRA IS A HAOS BAKUGAN.

WORLD:
DARKUS

Darkus Bakugan do their best fighting at night. They are known for their intimidating powers of destruction.

MASQUERADE'S HYDRANOID IS A DARKUS BAKUGAN.

WORLD:
VENTUS

If you've ever been caught in a hurricane, you know how damaging the power of wind can be. Ventus Bakugan are known for their speed, and their ability to blow their opponents right off the field!

SHUN'S
SKYRESS
IS A
VENTUS
BAKUGAN.

CLASS:
ROBOTALLIAN

These hulking metal beasts are definitely robot-like—
they're extremely loyal to their allies. But they feel
the pain of defeat, just like Bakugan with fangs and
claws do.

CLASS:
SERPENOID

If you have a fear of snakes, you'd better steer clear of the Serpenoid class! These giant serpents like to wrap their bodies tightly around an opponent—and then squeeze!

CLASS:
REAPER

Bakugan in the Reaper class are motivated by revenge, and they will attack with a fury unknown in the Bakugan universe. Maybe that's why every brawler's blood runs cold when Reaper stands on the field!

CLASS:
SAURUS

These hardcore brawlers are some of the toughest
Bakugan around. They might not be fast, but they
make up for their lack of speed with strength.

CLASS:
DRAGONOID

Dragonoids combine speed and agility with amazing power. They can fly high to target an opponent, and then destroy them with one blow.

CLASS:
FALCONEER

Their powerful wings and keen eyesight allow Falconeers to spot prey from afar and then swoop down for the attack.